That's Ridiculous, Said Nicholas

CHERYL TARAGIN

PAGE PUBLISHING, INC.
Conneaut Lake, PA

First originally published by Page Publishing 2021

ISBN 978-1-64628-573-0 (pbk)
ISBN 978-1-6624-3756-4 (hc)
ISBN 978-1-64628-574-7 (digital)

Printed in the United States of America

*To energetic independent little boys everywhere
and the mothers who love them,
and to Arielle, Rafi, and Shani.
I love you
more.*

*N*icholas Jon Paul Martin William Annabelle Tydings was born in the middle of a summer storm.

Father and Mother cooed with delight at their newborn baby boy.

"He has your pretty eyelashes and my curly blond hair," Father gushed with pride.

"And your cute button nose," Mother added with a contented smile. "I've never been so happy."

Happiness soon gave way to worry tinged with a drop of fear.

By the time he could count the gap between lightning flashes and thunderclaps, the boy had become quite the daredevil, often leaping in the air like a spawning salmon.

This did not please his parents or grandparents. Nicholas did this and Nicholas did that, they complained whenever Nicholas behaved badly.

Everyone called him Nicholas, that is, until the day he crashed into a wall, shattering a full-length mirror.

Father said the mirror was already cracked, but Mother couldn't get over the shock.

From then on, she always called Nicholas by his full name.

"Nicholas Jon Paul Martin William Annabelle Tydings, are you okay?!" Mother shrieked at the sound of breaking glass. The mirror looked much worse than Nicholas, who claimed he was perfectly fine. "Look at what you've done," Mother sighed, pointing to the broken mirror. "Seven years of bad luck because you don't know how to behave!"

"That's ridiculous," said Nicholas. "I was lucky not to get hurt."

And he moved on.

The first time Nicholas Jon Paul Martin William Annabelle Tydings heard his full name, he didn't believe it was his, especially the Annabelle part which sounded like the name of a girl.

"You're named after your great-great-grandfather, who came to this country with nothing but the shirt on his back and hope in his pocket," Father explained. "When the immigration clerk asked for his first name, he thought he meant his mother's name which was Annabelle. So, that became his new name."

"You mean because my great-great-grandfather didn't understand English, I have to go through life with the name of a girl? That's ridiculous," said Nicholas.

And he moved on.

One day, at a birthday party for Connie Colleen, his friend with a big backyard, Nicholas wandered into a neighbor's yard and couldn't find his way back to the party, not that he cared.

He passed the time chasing frogs and hunting for unusual rocks.

Meanwhile, Father and Mother became frantic.

When they finally found him, Mother hugged Nicholas tightly, breathing a huge sigh of relief, like a weight had been lifted from her shoulders.

"Nicholas Jon Paul Martin William Annabelle Tydings," Mother wailed, "you could've been eaten by bears!"

"That's ridiculous," said Nicholas. "There are no bears in this backyard."

And he moved on.

At heart, Nicholas wasn't a bad boy. He loved his parents and grandparents and wanted to grow up in a way that would make them proud.

But he also liked living life his own way.

Nicholas wished he could do both at the same time.

Sometimes that was impossible.

For example, Nicholas hated to bathe.

He especially hated the feeling of a soapy washcloth scrubbing against his smooth, silky skin.

Father and Mother insisted.

"Nicholas Jon Paul Martin William Annabelle Tydings, you'll grow mushrooms behind those ears if you don't wash daily," Mother warned in a tone that made him wonder if dirty ears could really grow mushrooms.

"That's ridiculous," said Nicholas.

And he wished he could move on.

The truth is Nicholas couldn't stay still.

The next day, during recess at school, Nicholas sat in an empty swing and began pumping his legs in and out, gradually gaining momentum. Soon he was soaring into the sky.

"I'm flying," Nicholas called out with glee.

He scooped up the food crumbs and dumped them in a bowl, remembering how kind Mother was to let him eat upstairs.

He had worked all day on a puzzle.

Mother didn't want him to starve.

Nicholas swept dust from the furniture and floor.

He straightened the covers of his bed.

His room looked much neater and cleaner.

Nicholas felt happy about his accomplishment.

Just then, Mother burst into his room.
A smile slowly crept across her face.

She plopped down in his rocking chair, motioning Nicholas to sit in her lap.

And he did.

"Nicholas Jon Paul Martin William Annabelle Tydings, your room is spotless," Mother gushed with pride. "See what you can do when you put your mind to it? You will do remarkable things one day!"

Mother hugged Nicholas gently.

"That's not so ridiculous," said Nicholas.

And he stayed.

About the Author

Cheryl Taragin is a proud mother and grandmother from Baltimore, Maryland. Her love for storytelling began at a very young age. This is her first book for children.

CPSIA information can be obtained
at www.ICGtesting.com
Printed in the USA
BVHW090941141221
624009BV00013B/1115

9 781646 285730